The cub reporters stood around the school entrance to watch what happened when the hard-hitting, tell-it-like-it-is Cub Reporter turned up in the pages of Miss Glitch's Gazette. The reaction started slowly...

BIG CHAPTER BOOKS

The Berenstain Bears and the Drug Free Zone

The Berenstain Bears and the New Girl in Town

The Berenstain Bears Gotta Dance!

The Berenstain Bears and the Nerdy Nephew

The Berenstain Bears Accept No Substitutes

The Berenstain Bears and the Female Fullback

The Berenstain Bears and the Red-Handed Thief

The Berenstain Bears
and the Wheelchair Commando

The Berenstain Bears and the School Scandal Sheet

Coming soon

The Berenstain Bears and the Galloping Ghost

The Berenstain Bears at Camp Crush

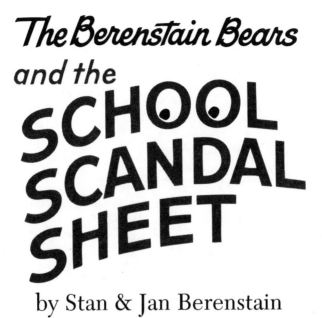

The Berenstain Bears
and the
SCHOOL SCANDAL SHEET

by Stan & Jan Berenstain

A BIG CHAPTER BOOK™

Random House New York

Library of Congress Cataloging-in-Publication Data
The Berenstain Bears and the school scandal sheet /
by Stan and Jan Berenstain.
   p. cm. — (A Big chapter book)
SUMMARY: Frustrated by their lack of artistic freedom on the staff of
the school newspaper, Brother Bear and his friends start an underground paper and discover some basic truths about freedom of the
press and responsibility.
ISBN 0-679-85812-1 (pbk.) — ISBN 0-679-95812-6 (lib. bdg.)
[1. Journalism—Fiction. 2. Newspapers—Fiction. 3. Schools—
Fiction.   4. Bears—Fiction.] I. Berenstain, Jan, 1923– . II. Title.
III. Series: Berenstain, Stan, 1923– Big chapter book.
PZ7.B4483Bejt   1994
[Fic]—dc20
93-45945

Manufactured in the United States of America 10 9 8 7 6 5 4 3 2 1

BIG CHAPTER BOOKS is a trademark of Berenstain Enterprises, Inc.

Contents

Chapter 1
The New Cub Reporters

It was a bright fall day in Bear Country, the kind of day that's made for after-school sports and games. When the bell rang at the end of the school day, most of the cubs had already made plans for the afternoon. Brother Bear, Cousin Fred, and Barry Bruin were ready for basketball on the school playground. Queenie McBear, Lizzy

1

Bruin, and Sister Bear had a soccer game at Grizzly Park. Harry McGill and Too-Tall Grizzly could hardly wait to start their next chess match at the picnic table in Harry's backyard.

But none of the cubs was in too much of a hurry not to stop first at the big bulletin board in the school lobby. On it was posted news they had been waiting for all week.

Too-Tall pushed his way through the crowd of cubs that had gathered in front of the bulletin board. He ran his eyes over the lists posted there and turned to smile at Harry McGill. Harry was watching eagerly from his wheelchair at the edge of the crowd.

"Did we make it?" called Harry through the noise of chattering cubs.

"Of course we made it!" Too-Tall called back with a grin. "Who would have the nerve to keep the two best chess players in Bear Country School out of the Chess Club?"

A few feet away from Too-Tall, Brother Bear was reading one of the lists. "Yes!" he cried. "Yes! Yes!" After yelling "Yes!" for the sixth time, he made his way back through the crowd to a group of friends waiting by the front door.

"We all made it!" he announced. "All six of us are in Journalism Club!"

"Yahoo!" shouted the cubs all together. There were high-fives all around.

Brother, Queenie, Cousin Fred, Babs, and Barry had been trying for years to get into Journalism Club. It met during the final school period every Friday. Each year they had listed their three club choices on cards and handed them in to their teachers. But none of them had gotten his or her first choice until now.

Ferdinand Factual, better known to some as Nerdy Ferdy, was especially lucky to have been chosen. That was because he didn't spend every year at Bear Country School. This year he was staying with his uncle, Professor Actual Factual, while his scientist parents went on a "dig" in Great Grizzly Valley.

There were all kinds of clubs to choose from at Bear Country School, including Chess Club, Computer Club, Soccer Club, Poetry Club, Music Club, and Carpentry Club, just to name a few. But the six cubs on the list for Journalism Club all wanted to write and publish a newspaper. Journalism Club was the perfect club for them, because its members wrote and published the weekly school newspaper, The Bear Country School Gazette.

"I can hardly wait for our first meeting," said Brother. "I don't know about you guys, but I want to cover sports. How about you, Ferdy?"

Ferdy Factual was so smart and so show-offy about it that Cousin Fred, who was pretty smart himself, said Ferdy gave nerds a bad name.

"I know so much about so many things," said Ferdy, "that I thought I might serve as

the paper's 'roving expert.' That way I could correct the errors the rest of you will surely make. How does that idea strike you?"

Ferdy got five thumbs down for his idea.

"In that case, I shall do science news," he said. "Not the baby science taught here at Bear Country School, but advanced science: chaos theory, modern particle theory—that sort of thing."

Barry and Queenie groaned.

"What about the rest of you?" asked Brother.

"Investigative reporting for me," said Cousin Fred. "You know, the story behind the story."

"I'd like to handle the arts section," said Babs.

Barry wasn't sure what he wanted to do. "Maybe I could help you on sports," he told Brother.

I'M GOING TO DO A SLAM-BANG NO-HOLDS-BARRED GOSSIP COLUMN!

Queenie hadn't spoken. She wasn't exactly a troublemaker, but she often seemed to be at the center of things when trouble happened.

"How about you, Queenie?" asked Brother.

"I'm going to shake up the tired old Gazette," said Queenie. "I'm going to do a slam-bang no-holds-barred gossip column."

Just then Sister Bear pushed her way through the crowd and came over to the group.

"Hey, Sis!" said Brother. "There were only six slots open in Journalism Club, and all six of us got in! You're looking at this year's cub reporters! Isn't that great?"

Sister just shrugged. The expression on her face was not a happy one.

"What's the matter?" asked Brother.

"I didn't get my first choice," grumbled Sister.

"Cheer up, Sister," said Cousin Freddy. "You're two grades below the rest of us. Only the older cubs get their first choices."

"I didn't get my second choice, either," said Sister.

"What *did* you get?" asked Queenie.

Sister wrinkled her nose as if she smelled something bad. "Poetry Club," she said.

"What are you griping about?" Babs scolded. "Poetry is great stuff. I'm planning to edit the arts page of The Bear Country School Gazette, and I plan to have a poem in every issue."

"You don't understand," said Sister. "I like poems. But in Poetry Club we'll have to write them. And I've never written a poem in my whole life!"

"There's always a first time," said Barry.

"That's right," said Babs. "And if you write a good enough poem, I just might print it in The Gazette."

"Really?" said Sister. Her eyes lit up.

"Maybe Poetry Club won't be so bad after all. At least I won't have to deal with that Miss Glitch again."

The other cubs looked at each other. Miss Glitch was the school's English teacher. She also happened to be in charge of The Bear Country School Gazette.

"Again?" said Cousin Fred. "When did you ever have to deal with Miss Glitch?"

"She filled in for Teacher Jane a couple of times," said Sister. "And she is tough. She's all sweetness and smiles, but if you don't do things exactly the way she says, she comes down hard on you. There are only two ways with Miss Glitch: her way, or the highway."

The cub reporters began to look worried. Maybe Journalism Club wasn't such a good idea after all. One of the reasons they had joined was to improve The Gazette. It certainly needed improvement. Everyone complained about it. It was boring. It was wimpy. And it had no real news.

"Well, I gotta go," said Sister. "Good luck with Miss Glitch. You're sure gonna need it! Remember what I said: her way, or the highway." Sister headed for the door.

Now the cub reporters looked really worried.

"If what Sister said is true, we could be in big trouble," said Cousin Fred.

"If Miss Glitch is the reason The Gazette is so boring," said Babs, "then we're not going to be able to do much about it."

"Maybe Journalism Club was a big mistake," said Barry.

"We could go to the office and say we've changed our minds," said Queenie. "Maybe they'll give us our second choices."

"Hey, cool it, guys!" said Brother. "We

haven't even had our first Gazette meeting yet and you're all panicking. Frankly, I don't think Miss Glitch is going to be a problem."

"What makes you say that?" asked Babs.

"Because I just happen to know what Sister's first choice for a club was," said Brother.

"What was it?" asked Barry.

"Journalism Club."

"Aha!" cried Queenie. "So she's just jealous!"

"Ah, yes," said Ferdy Factual. "That tainted fruit known as 'sour grapes.'"

The cub reporters all breathed great sighs of relief and went off to join their afternoon games and activities.

HER WAY, OR THE HIGHWAY!

Chapter 2
The Glitchville Gazette

Unfortunately for the cub reporters, what Sister had said about Miss Glitch turned out to be as true as could be.

As they came out of their first Gazette meeting that Friday afternoon, the cubs' faces were all kinds of unhappy. Brother and Queenie looked angry. Cousin Freddy looked sick. Babs and Barry looked stunned. Ferdy was trying to look bored but wasn't quite succeeding.

Behind them, Miss Glitch waved and called, "Good-bye, cubs. Have a good weekend. And don't forget our special afterschool meeting on Monday. I want to see how you're coming along on your first stories!"

The moment the door to Miss Glitch's classroom was closed, Babs let out a groan. "I can't believe it," she said. "Miss Glitch made all the decisions about my arts page!" She looked down at the notes she had taken. "I'm supposed to do book reports on Dick and Jane's New Puppy and The Bruin Twins at the Seashore. Those are first-grade books! And she wants a picture of flowers, and a poem...ugh...about the joy of poetry. She even gave me the first line:

"'Oh, the joy of words poetic.'

"She's got to be kidding! How am I going to find a rhyme for 'poetic'?"

"'Emetic' rhymes," said Ferdy.

"Yes, but what does it mean?" said Babs.

"'Emetic,'" said Cousin Fred, who read the dictionary for fun. "That which causes or stimulates vomiting."

"I like it," said Babs.

"Speaking of throwing up," said Ferdy, "I have been instructed to write a science story called 'Our Friend, the Water Molecule.' Yugh!"

The cubs left school and walked down the street toward home. Though it was another bright fall day, there seemed to be a dark cloud hanging over them.

"You think you've got trouble!" said

Our Friend The Water Molecule

Oh, the joy of words poetic

Brother Bear to Ferdy. "I'm the one who gets to cover sports the very same year Miss Glitch decides to cut sports down from a full page to a half page. Just so she can start a new section called 'Bear Country Weekly Wisdom'! What was that wonderful example of 'weekly wisdom' she gave you, Barry?"

Barry read from his notebook. " 'A penny saved is a penny earned.' "

Brother rolled his eyes. "For that she cuts sports in half?!"

"Don't complain," said Barry. "I'm the one who has to dig up enough 'weekly wisdom' to fill half a page."

Brother was certainly angry. But his anger was nothing compared to Queenie's. "You think that's bad!" she cried. "What about my gossip page? Miss Glitch turned it down cold! You heard her: 'Not a page, not a column, not a word of gossip will appear in The Bear Country School Gazette.' " Queenie was really upset. "What about freedom of the press? What about cubs' rights?"

"She did give you and Cousin Fred front-page news," said Ferdy.

"Front-page pap, you mean!" said Queenie.

"As much as I hate to side with the enemy," said Ferdy, "I must say I think Miss Glitch has a point. After all, gossip is, at best, a rather...trivial pursuit, shall we say?"

"Trivial pursuit? Why, you little four-eyed creep!" screamed Queenie. "How would you like me to make you eat that silly little hat of yours? And if you don't think I can do it..."

"Hold on, guys," said Brother. "Let's not get all mad at each other because we're mad at Miss Glitch. What we need to do is

HOW WOULD YOU LIKE ME TO MAKE YOU EAT THAT SILLY LITTLE HAT OF YOURS?

think of some way to improve things at The Gazette."

The others nodded. The cubs walked along in silence for a while.

"It's hopeless," said Babs finally. "Miss Glitch will never let us make any changes."

"Yeah," said Cousin Fred. "Miss Glitch rules The Bear Country School Gazette with an iron hand, and that's that."

"They ought to call it the Glitchville Gazette," sneered Ferdy. Suddenly he stopped and looked from side to side. "Hey, what happened to Queenie?"

The cubs turned to look behind them and saw Queenie halfway down the block. She was just standing there. When the cubs reached her, they saw that her eyes were wide open. She was staring off into space, lost in thought.

"What is it, Queenie?" asked Brother.

"Did you think of a way to improve The Gazette?"

Queenie looked at Brother and smiled. There was a strange twinkle in her eye. "Not exactly," she said. "I've got a better idea."

"What is it?" asked Cousin Fred.

"Meet me at the Burger Bear for shakes after dinner," said Queenie. "I'll tell you then. I've got to go work out the details."

Queenie turned and ran off down a side street toward her house. As the rest of the cubs headed home, they wondered what Queenie was up to.

Chapter 3
Birth of a Newspaper

That night the cubs were having milk shakes in their favorite booth at the Burger Bear.

"Well, Queenie," said Brother Bear. "What's your idea for The Bear Country School Gazette?"

"My idea for The Gazette," said Queenie, "is that it should have a front page full of

boring news about parent-teacher meetings,
new school employees, and upcoming quilt-
ing bees. There should be a half page of
sports and a half page of dopey wise sayings. And the arts page should have a bunch
of dull book reports and icky poems."

"Hunh?" said Cousin Fred. "That's
exactly the way Miss Glitch wants it!"

"If that's your idea of a good idea," said Ferdy Factual, "then I suggest you pay for all our milk shakes while we go home."

"Now, listen up," said Queenie. "We're going to write The Gazette exactly the way Miss Glitch wants it. But for a good reason."

"Okay," said Babs, "I'll bite. What's the good reason?"

"Because we're also going to write and publish a second newspaper," said Queenie. "And we'll do it exactly the way we want to."

"You mean an underground newspaper?" asked Babs.

UNDERGROUND?

"Underground?" said Barry, scratching his head.

"Go ahead, Fred," said Queenie. "Do your thing."

"Glad to," said Cousin Fred. "'Underground newspaper': a newspaper written and published outside the control of the established press."

"Exactly!" said Queenie. "It'll have hard-hitting news stories on the front page and a full page of sports. Babs can write anything she wants for the arts page, and Ferdy can do the same for the science page. In addition to covering sports, Brother Bear can be editor-in-chief and write editorials. And of course, I'll take care of the gossip page!"

The cubs looked at one another. It was certainly a fresh idea. And an exciting one!

Babs thought of the wonderful poems

and stories she would publish on the arts page. Cousin Fred thought of the fast-breaking news stories that he would put on the front page. Ferdy thought of writing the science page exactly the way he wanted to. Barry wasn't sure what he would write about, but he was glad it wouldn't be a bunch of boring old sayings.

The only cub who wasn't so sure about Queenie's idea was Brother Bear. He thought for a while and finally shook his head. "I think we could get into a lot of trouble with this underground newspaper," he said.

"But we won't," said Queenie. "No one will know who is publishing the newspaper, because we won't use our real names. We'll use pen names."

"Cool," said Barry. "I'll be 'Ballpoint.' Or maybe 'Fountain.'"

"Not that kind of pen name!" groaned Queenie. "Fred?"

"'Pen name,'" said Cousin Fred. "A made-up name that a writer uses instead of his or her real name."

"But we can't keep our names secret forever," said Brother.

"Don't worry," said Queenie. "By the time the school finds out who we are, we'll be heroes to all the cubs at Bear Country School. The school won't dare punish us."

That sounded pretty iffy to Brother. But he just nodded. Queenie seemed to have an

answer for everything. And the rest of the cubs all seemed to be on her side.

"But how will we print it?" Brother asked Queenie.

"I've already thought about that," she said. "Harry McGill can print it on his computer."

"What if he says no?" Brother asked.

"I'll convince him," said Queenie with a sly smile.

Brother still felt pretty nervous about the whole thing. He wondered if Queenie had come up with the idea just so she could write a gossip page. Or maybe just so she

could get back at Miss Glitch for coming down so hard on her.

And there was another thing that bothered Brother. Even though the underground paper was Queenie's idea and she seemed to have it all planned out already, she wanted him, Brother Bear, to be editor-in-chief! That was just like Queenie. She would come up with some new idea to change things. Then she would want someone else to take the blame for it if it flopped. Of course, if it succeeded, she would take the credit.

But as Queenie told the cubs about her ideas for the first issue of the underground newspaper, even Brother started to get excited about it.

"And I've got a terrific idea for the front page," said Queenie. "It will have the results of a survey of cubs about Bear

Country School teachers. I can see the headline: 'Students Grade Teachers: Cubs Finally Have Their Say!' We'll post notices here in Burger Bear and on the bulletin board in Biff Bruin's Pharmacy. They'll tell cubs to write down their comments and take them to the old hollow tree in the woods near school. We'll put a big cardboard box in the hollow tree to hold the comments. And they won't have to sign their names. That way cubs won't be afraid to say what they really think. We'll give Bear Country School the truth about itself for a change!"

The cubs loved Queenie's ideas. This new paper wasn't just going to be a challenge. It was going to be loads and loads of fun!

Brother thought Queenie's ideas were exciting. But he still hadn't made up his mind whether or not the newspaper was a good idea. After all, they hadn't even tried asking Miss Glitch if she would let them change some things about The Gazette. He knew that if he pointed this out to his friends, they would just say that Miss Glitch would never listen. They might be right. But Brother wasn't sure.

On the other hand, Brother did believe in printing the truth about things. And he sure didn't want to look like a wimp to his fellow reporters.

Then something popped into Brother's head, something that knocked everything else right out. He remembered the meeting with Miss Glitch earlier that day. He pictured Miss Glitch looking down her nose at him and saying, "Since sports news isn't as important as other news, I've decided to cut it to a half page...."

Brother got furious just thinking about it. His stomach churned with anger. The other cubs were all looking at him, waiting for his decision.

"Okay," he said at last. "Let's go for it."

"Right on!" shouted Queenie and the others.

"I have one last question," said Brother. "What will we call this new paper?"

Everyone thought.

"What was it you called us yesterday when we found out we all made Journalism Club?" Queenie asked Brother.

"You mean 'cub reporters'?" he said.

"That's it!" cried Queenie. "We'll call it The Cub Reporter!"

The cubs took their straws out of their shakes and held them together across the table like swords.

"All for one and one for all!" Queenie cried.

The other cubs at the Burger Bear wondered what was going on. They would be finding out soon enough.

Chapter 4
Powers of Persuasion

Queenie couldn't wait to put her plan into action. From the Burger Bear she went straight to Harry McGill's house on Boxwood Drive. Mrs. McGill let her in and took her down the hall to Harry's room. From behind the closed door came the click of a computer keyboard.

"Harry," called Mrs. McGill. "A friend's here to see you."

"Come on in, Too-Tall," Harry called back.

As Queenie opened the door, Harry looked up from his computer monitor and did a double take. "Too-Tall," he said with a grin, "you're looking more like your girlfriend every day."

"I'm not Too-Tall's girlfriend," said Queenie. "At least not this week."

"Pull up a chair," said Harry. "What can I do for you?"

Bursting with excitement, Queenie told Harry all about The Cub Reporter. She asked him if he would print it for them.

"That'll be a really cool first issue," said Harry. He imagined some of the cubs' comments about the teachers and smiled. Then he frowned. "But I don't know," he said.

"Miss Glitch and the other teachers aren't going to be jumping for joy about this. I could get in trouble."

"But you'll do it for your best friend's girlfriend, won't you?" said Queenie sweetly.

"You just said you aren't Too-Tall's girlfriend," said Harry.

"That's this week," said Queenie. "Next week I just might decide to be his girlfriend again."

Harry thought for a moment. He liked Queenie, even if he didn't think much of the way she treated Too-Tall. But...

He shook his head. "Sorry," he said. "Too risky."

Queenie got up to go. "Well, it's your decision," she said. "I certainly wouldn't want to talk you into doing something you don't really want to do."

Smiling slyly to herself, Queenie walked to the door. She had one more trick up her sleeve. And it was a doozie.

"By the way," she said as she reached for the doorknob. "Did Ferdy Factual tell you what Miss Glitch said when he asked her if he could write a computer column for the science page of The Gazette?"

"No," said Harry. "What did she say?"

"Oh, I'd better not tell you," Queenie said. "You'd just get upset." She turned the doorknob.

"Wait!" cried Harry. "Tell me what Miss Glitch said!"

"See, you're upset already," said Queenie. She opened the door.

"I AM NOT UPSET!" yelled Harry. "Please, Queenie..."

"Well, okay," said Queenie, closing the door again. "Miss Glitch said that computers are just fancy video games that turn cubs into empty-headed robots."

Queenie smiled. It wasn't true, of course. Ferdy hadn't even asked Miss Glitch about a computer column. But Queenie didn't care about that. All she cared about was

getting The Cub Reporter printed and into the hands of every cub at Bear Country School.

At first Harry looked shocked. Then he turned red with anger. "How dare she call me a robot!" he bellowed. "That does it! I'll print your newspaper, Queenie!"

"Oh, good," said Queenie. She came over to Harry and took a folded sheet of paper from her jacket pocket. "You can start with this," she said. "It's an announcement for our survey on teachers. I'll drop by tomorrow morning to pick up a few copies. Bye."

After Queenie had left, Harry sat staring angrily at the monitor.

"Empty-headed robots, huh! Well, old buddy," he said to the computer, "we'll show her!" He started typing Queenie's announcement into the computer.

Chapter 5
Canceled on Account of Rain?

The next morning Queenie took a big cardboard box out to the woods near school and placed it inside the old hollow tree. Then she picked up the announcements from Harry McGill and took them downtown.

On Saturday mornings, Biff Bruin's Pharmacy and the Burger Bear were always shorthanded. So it was the easiest thing in the world for Queenie to slip in and tack the announcements up on the bulletin boards without being noticed. Then she hurried home, grabbed her camera, and rushed out again to see if she could dig up some dirt for her new gossip page.

Queenie McBear wasn't the only cub hard at work that Saturday. But the others were not yet working on their Cub Reporter assignments. They were trying to get their Gazette stories finished first. They all realized that if they didn't get their work done for The Gazette, everyone would suspect them of being the writers of The Cub Reporter.

Midway through the morning, the bright fall day turned cloudy. Soon it began to drizzle. By noon it was really raining, and by mid-afternoon it was pouring.

The cub reporters gathered at the Burger Bear for a start-up meeting. They got their milk shakes and sat in their favorite booth watching the rain fall. Queenie was late, so they talked about Miss Glitch and their Gazette stories while they waited for her.

Queenie was a sight when she showed up. She was dripping wet. Rain had soaked right through her jacket and gotten under her hood. She looked like a drowned rat.

"What's that under your jacket?" asked Barry.

"My trusty camera, of course," said Queenie. "We photojournalists have to be ready to shoot at all times."

"In this rain?" said Babs.

"Neither rain nor sleet nor dark of night shall stay the photojournalist from her appointed rounds," said Queenie as she squished into the booth.

"That's what they say for the post office," said Ferdy.

"If it's good enough for the post office," said Queenie, "then it's good enough for me." She started to sneeze.

"I think you need a hot chocolate," said Cousin Fred. "Sit tight. I'll get it for you."

YOU'RE A TRUE AH-CHOO FRIEND !

Cousin Freddy returned with a steaming mug of hot chocolate and placed it in front of her.

"Here," he said, "take a slug of this. It's on me."

"Thanks, Fred. You're a true—AH-CHOO—friend!" She sipped the hot sweet drink. "Ahh!" she said. "That's better."

Then Queenie looked out at the rain. "Hey," she said. "Don't you guys realize what a problem this rain could be for us? If it keeps up, we won't get any comments for the big front-page story. And we need to collect them by Monday afternoon to get The Cub Reporter all written and printed up by Friday morning."

"That reminds me," said Brother. "How are we going to hand out The Cub Reporter, anyway?"

"I've got that all figured out," Queenie

said. "We'll fold it right into Friday's Bear Country School Gazette!"

"But then everyone will know that The Gazette reporters are writing The Cub Reporter, too," said Brother.

"Wrong," said Queenie. "Burt Bear, the printer, keeps the fresh Gazettes in an unlocked storage room overnight before shipping them to the school. Anybody could walk right in and mess with them."

The cubs were silent for a moment.

"Hmm," said Cousin Fred. "It just might work."

Brother Bear's eyes grew wide as he thought about it. Wow, what an idea! Using The Gazette to pass out an underground newspaper that criticized not only the school but The Gazette itself! It was brilliant!

There was no question about it—Queenie was on a roll. A very exciting roll—for truth, for cubs' rights, for freedom of the press. But at the same time, Brother could not quite shake the feeling that the roll just might be down a very steep hill with a sickening crash in store at the bottom. So before the Burger Bear meeting broke up, Brother squared his shoulders, looked Queenie in the eye, and said, "Queenie, just be sure to remember. I'm editor-in-chief. I must see all stories before they go to press."

"Even my gossip page?" asked Queenie.

"Especially your gossip page," said Brother.

"Don't sweat it, Chiefie," said Queenie. "Your wish is my command."

Chapter 6
Reaping the Harvest

Miss Glitch looked over her glasses at the cub reporters. "I think that brings our meeting to an end," she said. "Just hand in your stories. I'll edit them and perhaps add a few of my own. All in all, I think we're going to have a very exciting issue of The Bear Country School Gazette."

"You don't know how exciting," said Queenie under her breath. But it was almost loud enough for Miss Glitch to hear.

Babs dug an elbow into Queenie's side. "Stop clowning," she hissed. "You'll give us away."

"All right, cubs, you're dismissed," said Miss Glitch. "See you Friday afternoon."

Since the cub reporters were going to be putting out two newspapers, they really had their work cut out for them. As editor-in-chief, Brother went over all story ideas. Then he edited the stories and delivered them to Harry, who typed them into his computer.

Barry handed in a story criticizing Coach Grizzmeyer's old-fashioned style of football. When Babs handed in some pretty strong rap lyrics for the poetry section, Brother swallowed hard but said okay. Ferdy handed in a story criticizing the way Bear Country School was run. It was headlined "Bear Country School: A Perfect Demonstration of Chaos Theory." It was pretty harsh, and Brother wasn't sure about printing it. But it had some good points, too. After all, thought Brother, this whole thing was about cubs' rights and freedom of the press and "telling it like it is." Hey, he thought. That's what I'll call my editorial—"Telling It Like It Is."

The funny thing was that what Brother had been most worried about—Queenie's gossip page—turned out not to be a problem at all. It had some boyfriend-girlfriend stuff. It had some news about Bonnie Brown, who was off doing some modeling in Big Bear City. And it had the shocking information that Teacher Jane had a twin sister who worked for the Bear Country

Telephone Company.

But the big story, of course, would be the one headlined "Students Grade Teachers—Cubs Finally Have Their Say." Brother and his fellow reporters could hardly wait to see the results of their daring student survey.

What would the comments be like? Would there be enough? Would they be *printable?* Suppose, when Queenie got to the old hollow tree, the comment box was...empty!

Chapter 7
A Boxful of Poison

The cub reporters, except for Queenie McBear, walked through town and turned down Oak Street toward the old empty warehouse where they had agreed to meet.

Meanwhile, Queenie raced along a narrow forest path covered with fallen leaves. Around her the autumn air was crisp and the woods were every shade of red, yellow, and brown.

Queenie's heart pounded as she reached the old hollow tree. Would there be any comments in the box? The first issue of The

Cub Reporter depended on those comments. Without them The Cub Reporter
might as well be scrapped!

Holding her breath, Queenie tiptoed up
to the hollow tree. She reached inside. Her
hand touched the side of the box. She
slipped her hand over the edge and felt a
stack of papers. A huge pile!

YAHOO!

Queenie jumped for joy and yelled, "Yahoo!" which startled some birds and squirrels. Then she stuffed the comments into her backpack and hurried off down the path toward town.

Behind the empty warehouse, the other cubs were discussing the front-page story.

"I can't wait to see those comments," said Babs. "I hope there are some nasty ones!"

"Yeah," said Barry. "I hope we get some real nasty ones about Miss Glitch."

Brother didn't like the sound of that. "Hey, gang," he said. " 'Telling it like it is' is one thing. Being nasty is another."

Babs gave Brother a cold look. "Someone writing an editorial about truth in journalism should know that sometimes the truth is nasty," she said. "Besides, what about cubs' rights and freedom of the press?"

"Those things are very important," said

Brother. "That's why we're putting out The Cub Reporter. But there's such a thing as grownups' rights, too. And that includes teachers. There's more to freedom of the press than just shooting your mouth off."

"It sounds to me," said Ferdy Factual, "as if our editor-in-chief is getting a case of frigid pedal extremities, better known as 'cold feet.'"

"Better cold feet than mean, nasty, and unfair!" shouted Brother.

"There's no use arguing about it," said Cousin Fred. "Let's wait until Queenie gets here with the comments."

The cubs didn't have long to wait. Moments later, Queenie came running around the corner of the warehouse. Panting hard, she screeched to a stop in front of

the cubs. Her eyes sparkled.

"We did it!" she cried. "We got a zillion comments!"

"Let's see!" said the cubs.

Queenie unzipped her backpack and dumped the papers at their feet.

"Wow," said Barry. "Queenie, you're a genius!" He picked up one of the papers and began reading aloud. " 'Teacher Bob is a wimp. He lets Too-Tall get away with murder.' "

"Perfect!" cried Queenie. "That's just what we're looking for!"

"Now wait a minute," said Brother Bear.

"Listen to this," said Queenie. " 'Miss Glitch is the worst teacher in the universe. Correction: Miss Glitch is the worst teacher in the known universe. It may turn out that there's a worse one on some distant planet.' "

There were cries of "Yippee!", "Hooray!", "Terrific!"

"How about this one," said Cousin Fred. "Mrs. Bruinwell..."

Brother could see his whole life flashing before him. Especially the part where he was going to get expelled from school for being editor-in-chief of The Cub Reporter.

As it turned out, the results of the "Students Grade Teachers" survey reminded Brother of that old Clint Bearwood movie

The Good, the Bad, and the Ugly. A few of the comments were good, a few of them were bad, and most of them were downright ugly.

A FEW OF THEM WERE GOOD,

I like Mr. Carr because he doesn't give us homework over the weekend.

Mr. McNab is a good teacher because he lets you discuss instead of just telling you stuff.

Ms. O'bruin is a good teach— because

I like Mrs. Marple because she's pretty and wears cool clothes.

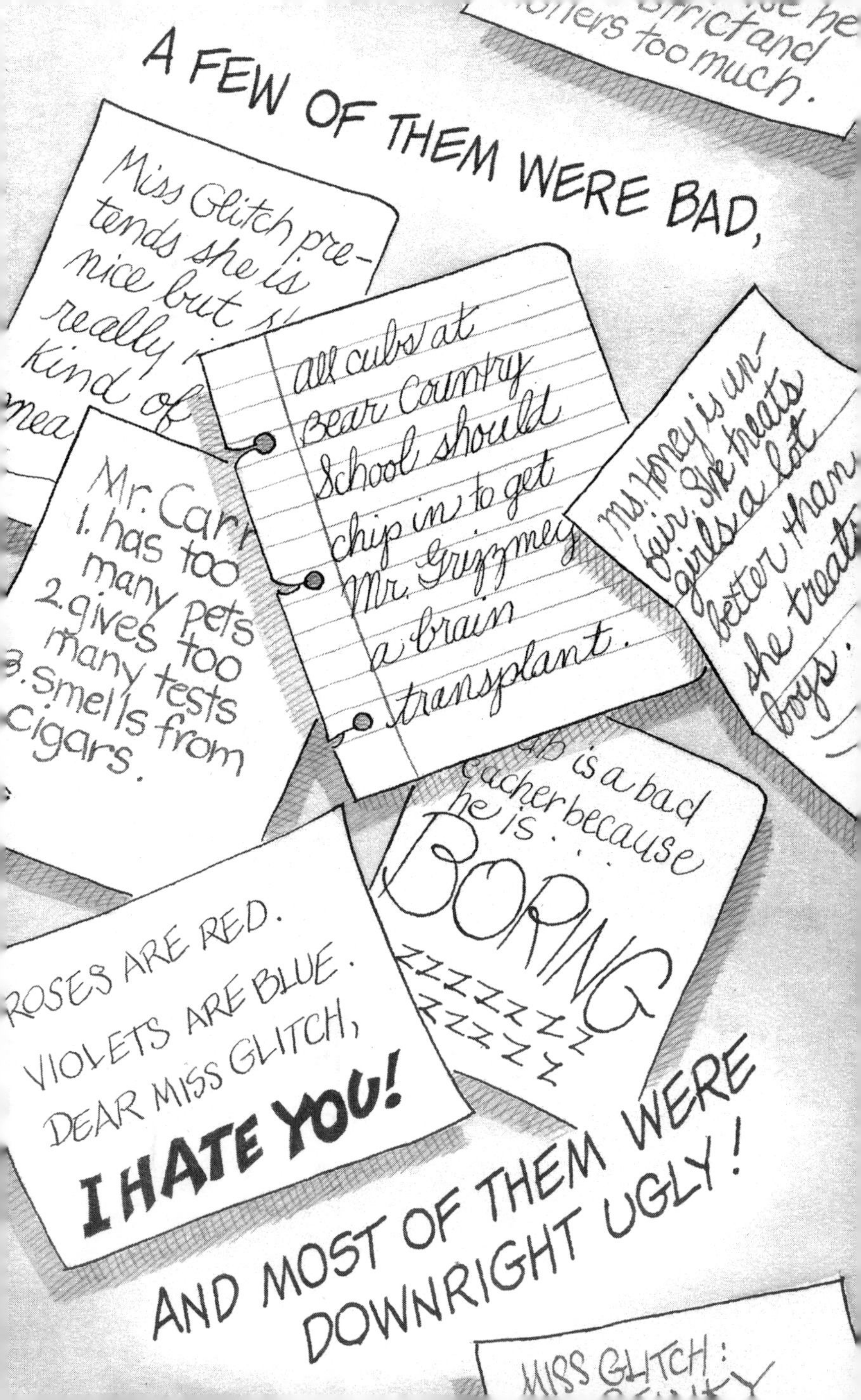

too much.
A FEW OF THEM WERE BAD,
Miss Glitch pre-
tends she is
nice but
Mr. Carr
1. has too
many pets
2. gives too
many tests
.Smells from
cigars.
All cubs at
Bear Country
School should
chip in to get
Mr. Grizzmey
a brain
transplant.
Ms. Honey is un-
fair. She treats
girls a lot
better than
she treats
boys.
is a bad
teacher because
he is...
BORING
ZZZZZZZ
ZZZZZZZ
ROSES ARE RED.
VIOLETS ARE BLUE.
DEAR MISS GLITCH,
I HATE YOU!
AND MOST OF THEM WERE
DOWNRIGHT UGLY!
MISS GLITCH:

Chapter 8
Queenie's Big Scoop

Queenie McBear walked through town one night later that week. She was still on the prowl for a really good story for her gossip-page—a real scoop.

It was beginning to look as if her gossip-page idea was going to be a big bust. All she had been able to come up with so far was some ordinary chitchat. It was all right as far as it went. But the page needed at least one really juicy story to put it over the top—something really eye-popping, something really shocking.

She'd had some pretty good ideas, but they hadn't worked out. She thought "Police Chief Bruno's Car Illegally Parked" would make a good headline. But when she checked the chief's car, it was parked behind the police station in the space marked "Chief." She even followed Ralph Ripoff around for a story. But all he did was check out the coin returns in the pay phones. That was no story. Ralph always did that.

Queenie headed home. Even if she found a story, it was too late to get it in the paper. Harry McGill was already hard at work typing up The Cub Reporter on his computer.

As Queenie passed the Red Berry, a popular restaurant, she happened to look in the front window. Wasn't that Teacher Bob inside having dinner with Mrs. Bob?

Queenie went to the window and raised her hand to wave. It was indeed Teacher Bob inside having dinner. He was seated at a table in a far corner of the room. The table was lit by a single candle. How romantic, thought Queenie.

Then she gasped. Teacher Bob was not with Mrs. Bob! He was with a teenager. And a beautiful teenager at that!

Queenie sneaked over to the corner of

the window and peered in. Teacher Bob was talking and smiling at the girl. The girl was smiling back at Teacher Bob. They seemed to know each other very well.

Wow! thought Queenie. Straight-arrow, goody-two-shoes Teacher Bob was out on a date with a teenager! What a story! What a scoop! What a scandal!

It was just the story Queenie needed to spice up her gossip page. And there still might be time. If she hurried, she could write up the story and get it to Harry McGill before he finished typing The Cub Reporter.

But what about Brother Bear? She had promised to show him all her stories before giving them to Harry. But there wasn't time for that. Besides, Brother was such a nervous Nellie he might try to argue her out of it.

What is a reporter's first duty? Queenie asked herself as she stood frozen at the restaurant window. The answer came in a flash: TO GET THE STORY!

She slipped her camera from her backpack and aimed it at Teacher Bob and his date. Click! The flash went off. Queenie ran.

Inside the Red Berry, Teacher Bob blinked and looked at the window. "What was that?" he said.

"They must be celebrating at another table," said the girl. "A birthday, maybe."

"But it came from outside, didn't it?" said Teacher Bob.

Teacher Bob and the girl both shrugged and went back to their dinners.

Chapter 9
Read All About It!

The day for passing out The Bear Country School Gazette and its secret cargo—The Cub Reporter—finally came. Nat Newshound, Selma Scoop, Teddy Testtube, Marilyn Muse, Homerun Homer, and I. M. Wright were all pretty nervous. Those were the pen names chosen by Cousin Fred, Queenie, Ferdy, Babs, Barry, and editor-in-chief Brother Bear.

The cub reporters stood around the school entrance to watch what happened when the hard-hitting, tell-it-like-it-is Cub Reporter turned up in the pages of Miss

Glitch's Gazette. The reaction started slowly. Then it grew and grew and grew until Brother and his staff knew they had a huge success on their hands...*and* a huge disaster!

The students loved The Cub Reporter! They loved it to pieces! The teachers, on the other hand, hated it. A couple of them, including Coach Grizzmeyer, tore it to pieces.

As much as they might have liked to take credit for their work, the cub reporters couldn't give away who they were. So they pretended that The Cub Reporter was as much a shock to them as it was to everyone else.

But when Brother came to Queenie's big scoop, he didn't have to pretend. The story about Teacher Bob was the biggest shock he had ever had.

The headline read, "Popular Teacher Dates Gorgeous Teenager." The story read, "What teacher whose name begins and ends with the letter 'B' was seen Tuesday night at the Red Berry whispering sweet nothings into the ear of a bee-yootiful young teenager? Naughty, naughty, Teacher B_b." The story was signed "Selma Scoop."

Brother threw his head back and shouted "QUE-E-ENIE!"

Queenie came running. "What's up?" she asked.

Brother was trying hard to keep calm. "Why didn't you show me this story before you put it in the paper?" he asked.

"There just wasn't time," said Queenie. "And the first duty of a reporter is to get the story."

"No," said Brother. "The first duty of a

reporter is to get the story *right!* And you've got it wrong!"

"I beg to differ, Chief," said Queenie. "You can see right here in the picture—"

"That's Teacher Bob's niece!" said Brother.

"Niece?"

"That's right, *niece,*" said Brother. "She's in the area looking at colleges. My mom had her over for tea last week."

Queenie looked as if she'd lost her best friend—herself! Now Queenie's whole life flashed before her—especially the part where she was going to be expelled from school for life.

Brother glanced over at the school entrance. The teachers were gathered around Mr. Honeycomb, the principal. Teacher Bob was among them. His face was a mask of fury.

DISGRACEFUL!

Chapter 10
Who Done It?

The first thing Mr. Honeycomb did was set up an investigation committee. Since a number of teachers had been hurt by The Cub Reporter, Mr. Honeycomb thought it was important to have a teacher on the committee along with himself and Mr. Grizzmeyer, the vice principal.

He called Miss Glitch's classroom, but a student answered. Miss Glitch was so upset about The Cub Reporter that she had gone home without even telling the front office.

So Mr. Honeycomb called Teacher Bob.

Teacher Bob said he would be glad to be on the committee because he was too angry to teach, anyway.

Within minutes, Mr. Honeycomb, "Bullhorn" Grizzmeyer, and Teacher Bob met in the principal's office to plan their investigation into The Cub Reporter. They spread out a copy of the underground newspaper on Mr. Honeycomb's desk.

"Disgraceful!" said Teacher Bob. "And right in the middle of The Gazette! How could this have happened?"

"I just called Burt Bear, the printer," said Mr. Grizzmeyer. "He didn't print it. He says someone must have sneaked into his storage room after The Gazette was finished and slipped The Cub Reporters into The Gazettes."

"Of course he didn't print it," said Mr. Honeycomb. "It isn't newsprint. It's computer paper. The Cub Reporter was typed on a personal computer."

Mr. Honeycomb and Mr. Grizzmeyer looked at each other. "Harry McGill," they said together.

"Harry McGill?" said Teacher Bob. "This doesn't seem like something Harry McGill would do on his own. He may have printed it, but someone else must be behind the whole thing."

"Easy," said Mr. Grizzmeyer. "Harry's best friend."

"Too-Tall?" said Teacher Bob. He shook his head. "Throwing bricks at windows is more his style. I can't see Too-Tall and the gang going to all the trouble to write and publish an underground newspaper. I can just barely get them to read."

"There's only one sure way to find out," said Mr. Grizzmeyer. "Let's get Too-Tall

in here for questioning."

Mr. Honeycomb reached for the switch on his intercom. "I'll have the school secretary call Too-Tall to the office," he said.

Moments later, Ms. Bearson's voice rang out loud and clear over the public-address system in Teacher Bob's classroom.

"Attention please, attention please: Too-Tall Grizzly, report to the principal's office."

Teacher Bob had made Brother Bear classroom monitor for the hour. Too-Tall looked at Brother and got up slowly. He was grinning.

"They can't pin this rap on me," he said. "Me and the gang have a perfect alibi. We're too stupid to put together a newspaper!" As he passed Brother, he whispered, "Harry told me all about it, Big Mr. Editor-in-Chief. Boy, are you gonna get it!"

Brother swallowed hard as Too-Tall left the room. Brother didn't know which was worse: how guilty he felt for hurting the teachers—especially Miss Glitch and Teacher Bob—or how foolish he felt for even thinking that he and his friends could get away with The Cub Reporter. He almost felt like going to the principal's office and telling the whole story. But he couldn't do

BOY, ARE YOU GONNA GET IT!

that without squealing on his friends.

Brother was lost in his troubled thoughts when Too-Tall returned to the room.

"Harry," said Too-Tall, "they want you in the office. Pronto!"

Harry wheeled himself swiftly across the room and into the hallway. Too-Tall wasn't grinning anymore. He was dead serious. He came close to Brother.

"No, you little creep," he said, "I didn't squeal on you and your underground friends. But if you got my chess buddy, Harry, in trouble, I'm gonna clean up the schoolyard with you one by one—girls included."

Brother couldn't look Too-Tall in the eye. It wouldn't be any more than we deserve, he thought.

Then he had another thought. What about Harry? Would Harry squeal?

GOOD GRIEF!
LISTEN TO THIS!

Chapter 11
A Heavy Burden

As Brother walked home from school that day, he was still wondering whether Harry McGill had squealed on the cub reporters. But as he neared the Bear family tree house, he began to wonder instead how soon Mama and Papa Bear would find out about The Cub Reporter and the huge mess that it had caused.

He didn't have to wonder long. When he got home, Papa was sitting in his easy chair reading the afternoon newspaper.

"Good grief! Listen to this!" said Papa just as Brother and Sister walked in the door. "Someone sneaked an underground newspaper into The Bear Country School Gazette!"

"No kidding," said Sister. Brother kept his mouth shut.

"And listen to this," said Papa. " 'Teacher Bob Denies Cub Reporter Story. When asked by our reporter for his comment, the accused teacher said, "That was no teenager! That was my niece!" ' "

"It *was* his niece," mumbled Brother.

Papa put down the paper and shook his head sadly. "What are cubs coming to these days?" He turned to Brother. "You're on The Gazette. You must be furious about this."

"Furious isn't the half of it," said Brother.

That night Brother lay in his bunk staring into the darkness. Sister leaned over the edge of the upper bunk and looked down.

"Can't sleep?" she asked.

Brother nodded.

"What's eating you?" asked Sister.

Brother thought of all the harm that The

WHAT'S EATING YOU?

Cub Reporter had done. He thought of the nasty student comments they had published. He thought of the horrible untrue story about Teacher Bob. He thought of the look on Teacher Bob's face when he read the story. He thought of poor old Miss Glitch being so upset that she had to leave school.

Suddenly Brother was pouring his heart out to Sister. He told her the whole story from beginning to end. About how Queenie had come up with the idea for The Cub Reporter and gotten him to be editor-in-chief. About Queenie promising to show him all her gossip stories before she gave them to Harry McGill. About how Queenie had slipped the Teacher Bob story past him. About how the whole thing had made him uneasy all along.

"Wow," said Sister when he had finished.

"You must feel awful."

"I've never felt so awful in my life," said Brother.

Sister tried hard to think of something that might cheer her brother up. "There was one good thing about The Cub Reporter," she said brightly. "The editorial about truth in journalism."

But then Sister frowned and shook her head. "But it did look kind of silly being in the same issue with Queenie's phony story about Teacher Bob."

"It sure did," said Brother.

Brother turned on his side so that he was facing the wall. He closed his eyes.

But he still couldn't sleep.

Chapter 12
In the Lions' Den

At school on Monday morning, Brother Bear kept looking up at the loudspeaker above the door in Teacher Bob's class. At any minute it might crackle to life with the sound of Ms. Bearson's voice calling him to the principal's office.

But it didn't.

Teacher Bob covered the weekend math homework, then the English homework. Still the dreaded loudspeaker was silent. It was beginning to look as though the big investigation had ended with Harry McGill. Harry must not have squealed!

As Teacher Bob talked, the cub reporters looked around the classroom at one another and winked. They were safe!

But then Teacher Bob closed his lesson book and made an announcement that sent chills down the spines of the cub reporters.

"As I dismiss the class for recess," he said, "I want the following cubs to stay behind: Babs Bruno, Barry Bruin, Ferdy Factual, Cousin Fred, Queenie McBear, and Brother Bear. Class dismissed."

Brother's heart sank. Teacher Bob had

just named the entire staff of The Cub
Reporter!

Too-Tall passed Brother on the way to
recess. He had a wicked grin on his face.
"Now you're gonna get it!" he sneered.
"When old Bullhorn gets through with you,
you won't be worth cleaning up the schoolyard with."

Harry McGill was right behind Too-Tall.
Brother glared at him and said, "You
squealed!"

"No, I didn't!" said Harry. "Honest!"

"Liar!" said Brother.

When the rest of the cubs had gone, Teacher Bob led the cub reporters down the hallway to a large meeting room. Brother was in for another unpleasant surprise.

At a big round table sat not only Mr. Honeycomb, Mr. Grizzmeyer, and Miss Glitch, but all of the cub reporters' parents, including Mama and Papa Bear. All except

for Ferdy Factual's parents. Actual Factual had come instead. He didn't look at all pleased about having been called away from his research.

The cubs joined the grownups at the round table. Mr. Grizzmeyer had a copy of The Cub Reporter in front of him. He cleared his throat to speak.

"I'll get right to the point," he said in his deep, gruff voice. "We know that you cubs wrote and published The Cub Reporter. What we don't yet know is exactly who wrote what parts of it." He looked down at the paper and then back at the cubs. "Which one of you jokers is Nat Newshound?"

Silence.

"Well, speak up," said Mr. Grizzmeyer.

"Er...uh...that would be me," said Cousin Freddy.

"And who is Marilyn Muse?"

Babs Bruno raised her hand.

"I. M. Wright?"

For a second, Brother felt as if every muscle in his body were frozen stiff. Then he felt his hand go up slowly.

When Mr. Grizzmeyer had finished naming the cub reporters, he leaned back in his

WHICH ONE OF YOU JOKERS IS NAT NEWSHOUND?

chair and folded his thick arms across his chest. "Now a question for all of you," he said. "Why in the world did you do it?"

Silence again. You could have heard a pin drop in the room.

At first none of the cub reporters wanted to speak. But before long they were all defending themselves at once—especially Queenie, who was on her feet making a big speech about cubs' rights and freedom of the press.

Brother had heard more than enough from Selma Scoop. "Cool it, guys!" he said.

"And you, Queenie—sit down and shut up!"

Then he turned to Mr. Grizzmeyer. "We did it because we were angry," he said. "I was angry about the sports page being cut in half, and Queenie was angry about her gossip-page idea being turned down. We were all angry about being told exactly what to write. We didn't have any freedom at all at The Gazette.

"I guess we didn't bother to think about how much freedom we should have or how to use it. Things got out of hand. That was my fault, because I was editor-in-chief. I

WE DID IT BECAUSE WE WERE ANGRY.

still believe in truth in journalism. But I know that it doesn't mean being nasty. And it sure doesn't mean printing crazy stories about bears' private lives without checking the facts first." He glared at Queenie.

"Well, it's good to hear someone talking sense," said Mr. Grizzmeyer. "But that doesn't mean there won't be any punishment. Not only did you cubs publish nasty and false stories, but you misused The Bear Country School Gazette to distribute your paper. You also trespassed in Burt Bear's storage room."

Mr. Grizzmeyer called an end to the meeting. He told everyone, parents included, to come back at the end of the school day to hear what the cub reporters' punishment would be.

Mama and Papa walked out into the hall with Brother. Neither of them spoke.

Brother was so ashamed and embarrassed that he didn't know what to do or say. So he started complaining about Harry McGill.

"That no-good snitch!" he growled. "That lousy squealer! Wait'll I get my hands on him!"

"Now, just a minute," said Mama. "Harry McGill didn't tell on you."

"Sure he did," said Brother. "He was the last cub questioned by Grizzmeyer."

"I know Harry didn't tell on you," said Mama. "Because I did."

Brother stared up at Mama. "You?" he gasped.

Mama nodded. "Sister was so worried about how bad you felt all weekend that she finally told me the whole story. She thought I might be able to help. I decided that the best thing to do was to call Mr. Honeycomb so that we could settle the whole thing right away."

Brother couldn't believe it. His own mother! Turning him in as if he were a common criminal!

Brother felt tears in his eyes. He turned and ran. Down the hall he went, through the front door and into the crowded schoolyard. He dashed across the hopscotch courts and right through a dodgeball game. He ran across the baseball diamonds. When he reached the edge of the playground, he slipped through a hole in the fence and disappeared into the woods.

Chapter 13
A Good Friend

Brother Bear ran along a narrow path through the woods until he reached his Thinking Place. There he sat among the rocks and thought. Usually he used his Thinking Place to solve problems, but now all he could think about was what a big problem he had.

He was editor-in-chief of an outlaw newspaper. It might be the worst newspaper published in Bear Country history. And his own mother had turned him in! It looked as

if his worst fears could really happen. He wouldn't blame them if they did expel him. How could he go back there? How could he go to that after-school meeting and face his horrible fate?

Just then Brother heard some twigs snap in the woods nearby. Then a strange creaking sound. A voice called, "Brother! Are you there?"

It was Harry McGill's voice. Brother jumped up and saw Harry in his wheelchair at the edge of the clearing.

"Hey, give me a hand," called Harry. "My

wheelchair is all tangled up in this vine."

Brother went over to help. As he untangled the vine from Harry's wheelchair, he asked, "What are you doing all alone out here in the woods?"

"I came looking for you," said Harry. "I saw you run out of school and across the schoolyard. I figured something pretty bad must have happened. I got worried."

"You did?" said Brother. "Even after I accused you of squealing?"

"Sure," said Harry. "Don't worry about that. I probably would have thought the same thing if I were you. By the way, did you find out who squealed?"

Brother told Harry how Sister had told Mama and how Mama had called Mr. Honeycomb.

"And that's why you ran away?" asked Harry.

Brother nodded.

"Look," said Harry. "I know you're real upset right now. But you've got to realize that your mom did the best thing she could. The school would have found you guys out anyway. Better to get the whole thing settled right away than to drag it out forever."

Brother sighed. "I guess you're right," he said. "But I still don't see how I can go back there. They're going to expel me!"

"I doubt that," said Harry. "But whatever

they do, you can't stay out here forever. Besides, you're already expecting the worst. So things can't get any worse than you expect!"

Brother smiled for the first time since The Cub Reporter had come out. The two cubs started back down the narrow path.

"To tell you the truth," Harry said, "I could use some help getting back. These vines are murder."

Chapter 14
Facing the Music

As it turned out, the cub reporters' punishment was not as bad as Brother expected. In fact, it wasn't even half as bad as he expected.

No one got expelled. No one got suspended.

The cub reporters would have to miss recess for one week. During recess they would work on the next edition of The Bear Country School Gazette.

Ordinarily, that would have seemed like a pretty bad punishment. But The Bear Country School Gazette wasn't going to be

the same old boring Glitchville Gazette.

At the meeting, right in front of everyone, Miss Glitch admitted that she had been too strict with The Gazette reporters. She said that she loved The Gazette so much that she had forgotten that it really belonged more to the cubs of Bear Country School than to her. She was willing to give the reporters more freedom. In the future she would supervise them without telling them what to write.

Brother Bear felt light as a feather as he walked home with his family. Things hadn't turned out so bad after all. Mr. Honeycomb had even praised Brother's editorial about truth in journalism.

As the Bears walked along, Brother talked about the changes he wanted to make at The Gazette. "The first thing I'm going to do," he said eagerly, "is get rid of that awful 'Bear Country Weekly Wisdom' section."

"Now hold your horses," said Papa Bear. "I think you ought to keep that as part of your punishment." He laughed.

"Yes," said Mama, going along with the joke. "And I know just the wise saying for the next issue."

"Do you mean, 'All's well that ends well?'" asked Brother with a smile.

"Not exactly," said Mama. "I was thinking of something more like, 'Look before you leap.'"

Brother's cheerful smile turned into a

sheepish grin. "Oh, yeah," he said. "That's a good one, too."

As troubled as the day had been, Mama, Papa, and Sister couldn't help laughing. Even Brother chuckled a little.

When the Bear Family's tree house came into view, Brother was reminded of another old saying: "Home is where the heart is."

They've got that right, thought Brother as he led the way up the front steps.

Stan and Jan Berenstain began writing and illustrating books for children in the early 1960s, when their two young sons were beginning to read. That marked the start of the best-selling Berenstain Bears series. Now, with more than 95 books in print, videos, television shows, and even Berenstain Bears attractions at major amusement parks, it's hard to tell where the Bears end and the Berenstains begin!

Stan and Jan make their home in Bucks County, Pennsylvania, near their sons—Leo, a writer, and Michael, an illustrator—who are helping them with Big Chapter Books stories and pictures. They plan on writing and illustrating many more books for children, especially for their four grand-children, who keep them well in touch with the kids of today.